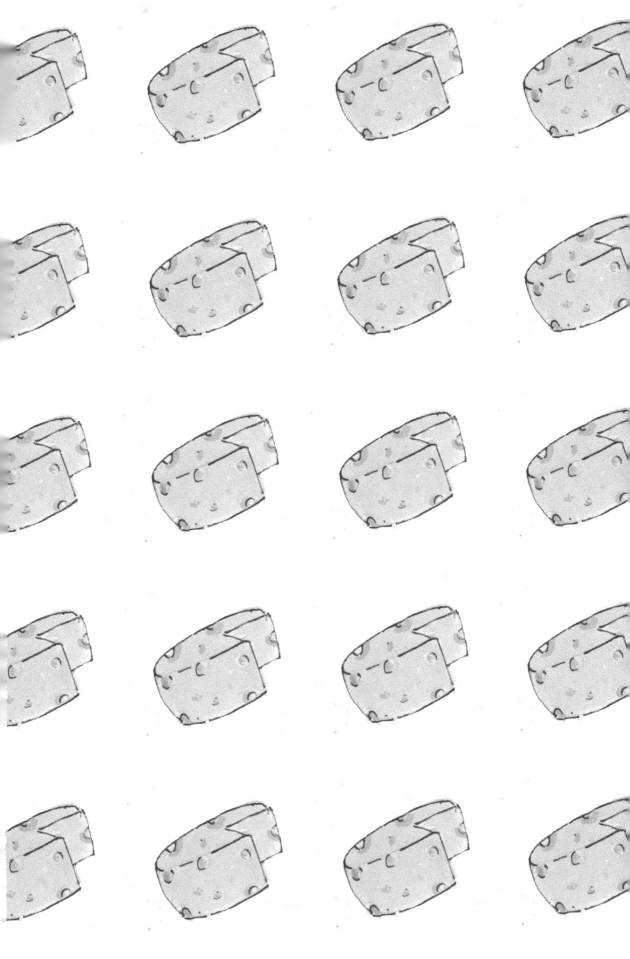

For Larry and Anne Rogers, my parents, who gifted me
with the freedom to imagine and create.
— Laura Kirkland

For Mom, Wynn, Asher and Georgia, all of whom have
taught me to use my imagination.
— Michael Albanese

First published by The Weight of Ink in December 2020
Written by: Michael Albanese
Illustrated by: Laura Kirkland

Created in The Town at Trilith, Fayetteville, Georgia
Printed in the United States of America

Please visit guardianofthegroceries.com and TheWeightofInk.com

THE WEIGHT OF
INK

GUARDIAN of the GROCERIES

written by Michael Albanese

illustrated by Laura Kirkland

Henry was bored.

Sure, it was a beautiful day, but as he sat on the front steps of his house, he craved an adventure.

Henry's mother came outside with a plate
of freshly baked chocolate chip cookies
(his favorite).

"It's okay to be bored sometimes," she
replied. "**BUT I DO** have an adventure for us."

"You do?" Henry jumped up and shoved one of
the cookies into his mouth. "What?"

"The grocery store!"
she exclaimed.

"The grocery store?" Henry whined. "That is the most boring place of all!"

"Anything can be an adventure if you just use your imagination," she said. "Let's go!"

As they approached the Star World grocery store, Henry started to have a change of heart. Who knows what adventure would be waiting for him?

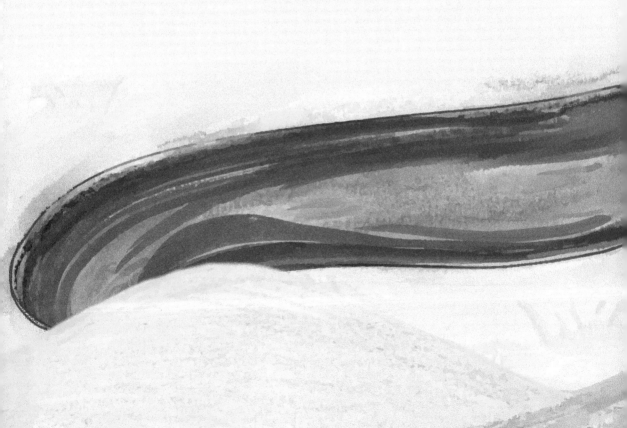

Together, Henry and his mother rolled up and down the aisles, adding items to the cart and double-checking their grocery list.

"Henry, I have to find a few more things," his mother said.

"Will you **guard our groceries?**"

Just then, the Store Manager approached Henry with a metal colander.

"If you're going to guard the groceries, you'll need a helmet," the man said.

"A helmet?" Henry was curious.

"Captain, I've flown from one side of the grocery store to the other and I've seen a lot of strange stuff," the manager said as he handed Henry the colander.

CAPTAIN? Henry thought to himself as he placed the colander on his head.

Suddenly, all the lights clicked off. The shopping cart rattled, hummed and hovered.

"Whoa!" Henry yelled as a bubble of glass formed around him.

A microphone extended from the helmet in front of his mouth. To his amazement, a throttle and a large red button appeared in front of him.

"Attention StarWorld Shoppers, this is Mission Control. We are now entering the Marketsphere."

From the inside of the helmet, Henry heard a mysterious voice. "Captain, what are your coordinates?"

Henry looked around. "Umm... aisle eight?" he said.

"Breakfastus Maximus was seen on aisle six. Prepare to engage."

Henry soared down the aisle at heart-racing speed. He heard a terrible growl and there he was: the dreaded Cereal Monster, a villain made of giant, family-sized cereal boxes!

When the grainy giant spotted Henry,
he hurled boxes of cereal at him. They
buzzed by the cartpod like colorful,
cardboard rockets.

"Prepare to launch lactomissles," instructed Mission Control as a red button rose from the control panel.

"Fire!"

Henry pressed the magical red button, launching a stream of milky missiles. The breakfasty beast collapsed on the floor in a heap of wet, soggy boxes.

Henry flew past Mission Control.

"Success, Captain!" the manager said as he waved at Henry. "But, we have another intruder in the dairy aisle!"

With great courage, Henry yanked the throttle. As he gained speed, he saw the dangerous Cheesyclops, a gooey monster made of sticky, stinky cheese.

The Cheesyclops stared at Henry with his one menacing eye. As the Muenster monster reached for the Cartpod, Henry raced by, avoiding a mozzarella mess!

"Cheese Melter loaded," advised Mission Control.

As Henry flew back toward the Cheesyclops, he pressed the red button, releasing a fiery blowtorch. The monster melted instantly into a gigantic blob and oozed all over the floor.

"Clean up on Aisle One!"
Henry declared with a victorious smile.

"Terrific mission,
Captain. But we have one
more invader to defeat.

This one is the
scariest of them
all!"

As Henry flew across the marketsphere, he saw a gnarled tree-like shadow lurking in the produce department.

"Broccolisaurus straight ahead!" warned Mission Control.

It was the most dreaded of the marketsphere monsters! A giant broccoli stalk with beady eyes made of ... **could it be**, Captain Henry thought?

Yes! Toasted almonds!

Henry tried to race past the crunchy creature, but the Broccolisaurus grabbed hold of the Cartpod with its frightening fingers.

"**Eat me! Eat me!**" yelled the ghastly green goliath as it shook the Cartpod. Henry tumbled dizzily inside. "Nooooooo!" he yelled.

Then, suddenly, everything went completely dark.

It was quiet.

Too quiet.

Through the darkness, from far away, Henry heard the sweet, familiar voice of his mother.

"Earth to Henry!"

Henry snapped out of it, surprised to see they were in the checkout line already.

That night when Henry sat down for dinner, guess what ended up on his plate? That's right—broccolisaurus! He heard the words ringing in his ear, "Eat Me!"

Henry thought to himself, "I'll show that broccoli who's boss!"

He took a big bite of the vegetable and said,
"Wow, Mom! This is actually really good!!"

His mother smiled and gave him another helping
of the little green monsters.

Later, when he went to bed, Henry thought about his adventures. He knew his mother was right: it really is okay to be bored sometimes.

Anything can be an adventure if you just use your imagination.

MICHAEL ALBANESE is a writer, entrepreneur and coffee aficionado. After many years adventuring in New York City and Los Angeles, he relocated to Georgia to help pioneer a creative community in South Atlanta. Michael lives and dreams with his wife, actress Wynn Everett, and their two imaginative daughters.

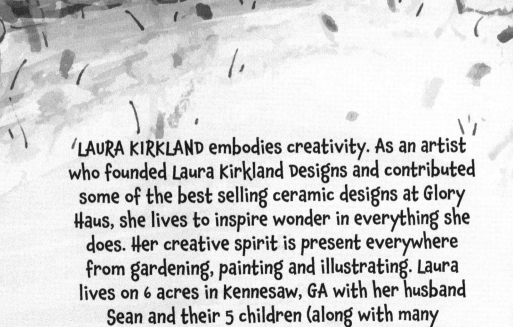

LAURA KIRKLAND embodies creativity. As an artist who founded Laura Kirkland Designs and contributed some of the best selling ceramic designs at Glory Haus, she lives to inspire wonder in everything she does. Her creative spirit is present everywhere from gardening, painting and illustrating. Laura lives on 6 acres in Kennesaw, GA with her husband Sean and their 5 children (along with many chickens!). This is her first children's book.

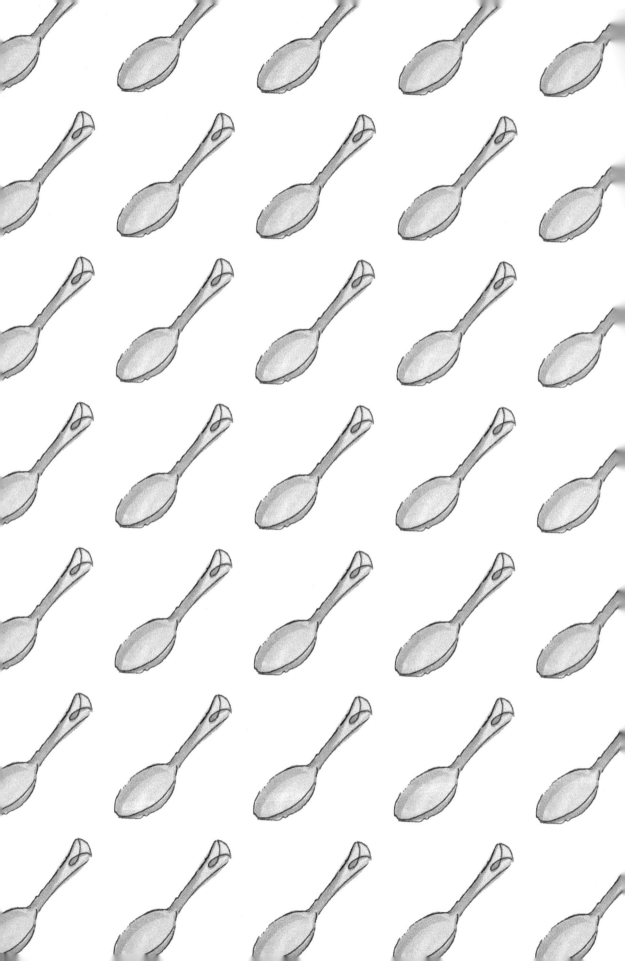

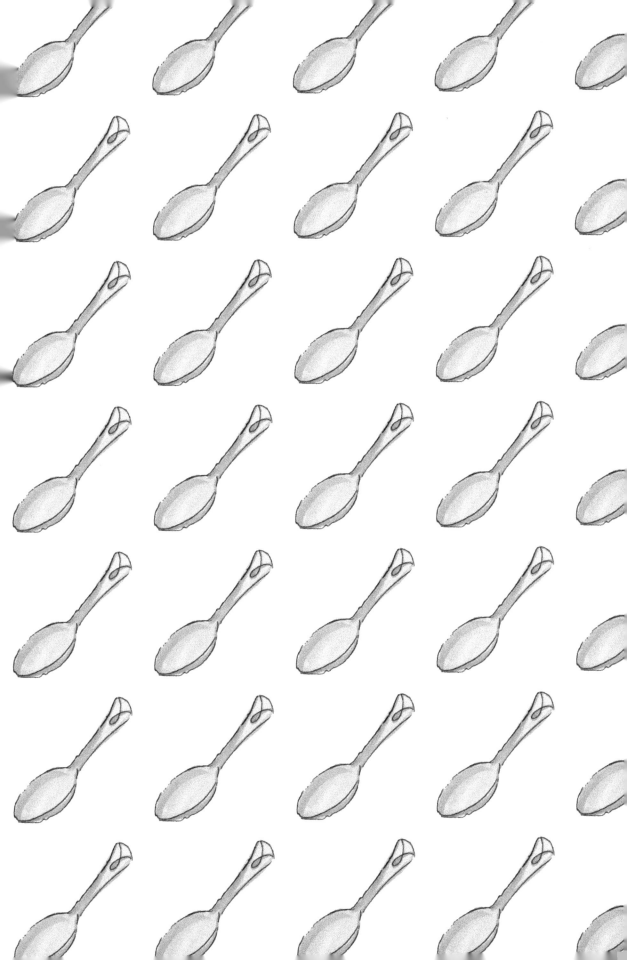

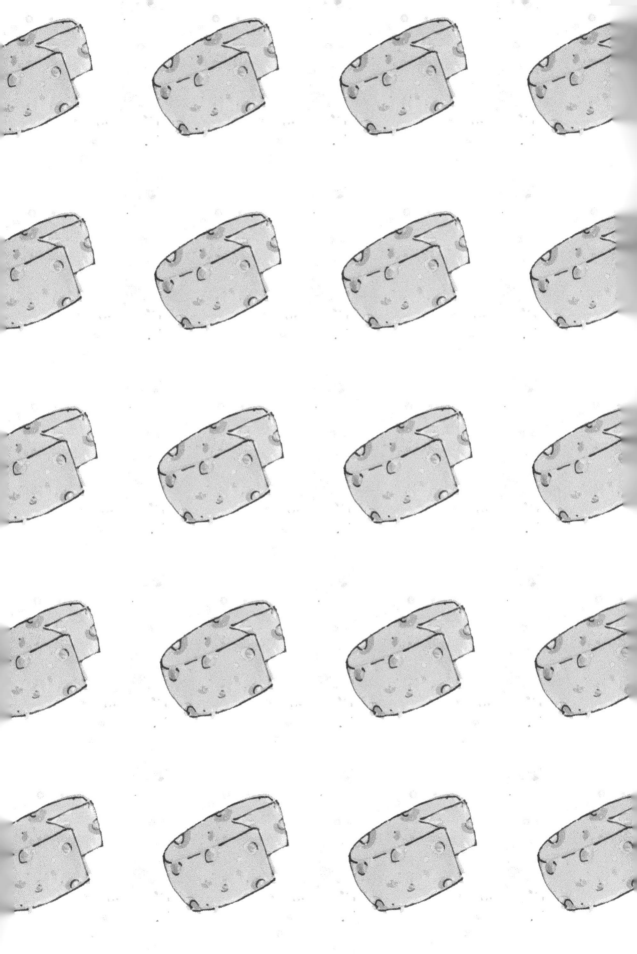

CPSIA information can be obtained
at www.ICGtesting.com
Printed in the USA
LVHW071754300621
691575LV00006B/270

9 781732 898721